Dear Reader,

On behalf of myself and the other contributing authors, I would like to welcome you to the eighth Open Door series. The books in this series are written and designed to introduce new and emergent readers to the writings of many bestselling authors who have sold millions of books worldwide. We hope that you enjoy the books and that reading becomes a lasting pleasure in your life.

Warmest wishes,

Patricia Scanlan

Patricia Scanlan
Series Editor

Please visit www.newisland.ie for information on all eight Open Door series.

Chapter One

I have not thought about that summer in the longest time.

Well, that is not quite true. It lingers, always, even in ways I am no longer aware of. But that is different from thinking about it. It is like a shadow. Something that is barely there. Most days it is hardly visible. Like an angel on my shoulder.

I met you in that Dublin hotel three days after my sixteenth birthday. You had just turned twenty. It was my first time to live away from home, my first ever summer job. Dad had put me on the bus at midday, pressing some coins into my hand as I boarded. 'Ring when you get there,' he said. 'There is a phone box in the main square, just beside the bus stop.' I nodded. 'Take care.' He kissed me on the forehead and we waved to each other as the bus left the city centre. I had never travelled such a distance on my own before. Although the village was only twenty miles north of home, it felt very different. The bus passed field after field of green. Houses were few and far between. There were no streets, not like the ones I was used to. And where, I wondered, had all the people gone?

When we pulled into the village square, suddenly there were people everywhere. Kids carried buckets and spades, sunburnt adults sat drinking pints outside the pubs. I could taste the salty tang of the sea. I was hot and sticky as I lugged my suitcase out of the bus, worrying about how far I had to walk. There was a line of people waiting outside the phone box. I decided I wasn't going to wait. I followed the bus driver's directions to the hotel, but I was panicky. I still feel that way when I am afraid of getting lost.

I found the door marked 'Staff Only' easily enough, and pushed it open. I struggled with the bag whose handles had dug their way into the soft flesh of my palms. The roots of my fingers had turned purple and ugly. I dared to look up at last, and you smiled.

'Hi,' you said. 'Miriam?' your voice lilted towards the North of the country.

'Yes,' I said. I remember feeling uncertain. I was not sure that I liked someone knowing my name before I knew theirs.

'I'm Marie-Claire,' you said. 'Patricia asked me to keep an eye out for you. We are roommates.' You tossed your hair, smiled at me, and tucked one long, blonde strand behind your ear. I noticed how green your eyes were. Your name was sophisticated, French, romantic somehow, and generous in the way mine was not. 'Miriam' was severe and old-fashioned. I hated my name in those days. I thought it sounded mean.

'Oh,' I said.

'Patricia will be back around five.' You smiled again, encouraging me. 'I can show you our room, if you like.'

Our room. I had never shared a room before. My house was crowded with brothers, big creatures who fought and made noise and needed to be cleaned up after. But I did have my own bedroom. It was tucked away at the back of the house. It was large enough for a single bed and a kitchen chair and three bookshelves. But at least those things were mine, and did not need to be shared with anyone else.

You did not wait for me to reply. You just led the way through that long kitchen to the stairs. I saw the scrubbed tables, the hard benches, the thick white plates piled at one end. There was a smell of sour milk. A shaft of sunlight showed a trail of salt or sugar across one of the tables, like the path of some large snail.

I followed you up the stairs to a narrow landing, then down a corridor with grey doors on both sides. You stopped outside number five. The number had slipped downwards. It needed a nail or a screw at the top corner to keep it in place. Dad would have shouted for Michael to fix it. He would never have approved of such sloppiness.

'In here,' you said, and pushed hard with one shoulder. The door swung open into a small room. Two bunk beds took up the entire wall on the left. On the right, there was a shelf, a mirror and a wardrobe. A small window separated the bunks from the rest of the room. The thin curtains were faded blue, patterned with silver moons. Later, I noticed that they did not meet in the middle.

'The bottom bunk is yours.' You opened the wardrobe door. Exactly one half of the hanging space was filled, as were four of the eight shelves. I remember noticing all the peeling surfaces that. I think. My silence was not what you had expected. You could not have known of the problems I had with speaking out and standing up for myself. The metal hangers chinked off one another gently.

'The bathrooms are at the end of the corridor, down that way.' You pointed and I knew you were about to leave. I needed to speak quickly, to say something, anything. I knew that I must have seemed odd. Mother would have told me not to be so rude.

'Great, thanks,' I managed, just as you opened the door and were about to step outside, away from me. 'Thanks for showing me. Is it okay working here?'

A wide grin lit up your face. Your eyes were even greener when the smile reached them. You seemed hopeful. Even then, I knew that look. So I had not disappointed you. Not completely, at least.

'Yes, it is,' you said, nodding. 'It is good fun. There is a really good bunch working here now. More boys than girls, too.'

More boys than girls. I was used to that. But brothers did not count, not even four of them. Not in the way you meant.

'What are you doing?' I asked. 'I mean, what job did they give you?'

Dad had explained that I had a position at the hotel until September, when school started again. That is all they told him. He said that when I got there they would 'assess' my 'suitability' for the kitchen, or the reception, or the café. Whatever they thought best. The way Dad said 'assess your suitability' told me how strange the words felt in his mouth. Drills and saws and hammers were what he knew. Not words that slipped away from him, lurking around the corners of his understanding, hiding their true selves. Suddenly, it became important to know how *your* suitability had been assessed. So I asked you, and your face changed. You looked like you could not believe your own good fortune.

'Jammy number,' you said, shaking your head. 'Wee Phyllis from reception had to go home for a funeral. I got to stand in for her.' You shrugged. 'I was the first of the temp staff to arrive. I think he was panicking. Barry, I mean, the manager.'

I loved your accent, the words you used that I had never heard before. I hung on to all of them. 'And do you like the work?'

'It is fine. Easier than waiting tables, that is for sure. I have waitressed for two summers now, back in Donegal. But I will not be in reception for long.

Barry just needed someone in a hurry and I fitted the bill.'

I nodded. I could see why. Besides the beautiful blonde hair and green eyes, you looked as though you knew your stuff. Like the right things to say, the ways to make unhappy customers happy. I could see how your smile would bring others to you, how people would want to be in your presence. I'd only felt that once before, with a teacher in primary school. She was younger than all of the others. She was pretty. All of us girls wanted to sit beside her, to do the jobs that she gave to the favoured few, over and over again. But the rest of us never lost hope. We believed that we would be the chosen ones some day. All we had to do was wait.

'Come on,' you said, looking at my battered suitcase. It was old and shabby. It suddenly made me feel ashamed. 'Leave all of that and I will show you around. You can unpack later.'

Do you remember showing me the hotel's three long corridors, the café, the gift shop? Afterwards, we made our way outside, through the grounds and down the long slope to the sea. You greeted people as they passed, smiled and stopped every now and then for a chat. That is how I met Brian and Gary, and Tom too, I think. But they hardly glanced at me. Their eyes were on you. Sometimes, even when they had walked on, I had that sense of people looking back at us, at you, over their shoulders.

When the path narrowed, you led the way to the beach and I followed. By the time we reached the sand, I understood all the differences between us. Your hair was straight and sleek. Your jeans were a perfect fit and you were the perfect height. Not too small, not too tall. Above all, you moved with an ease and a confidence that I could never copy.

Suddenly, you stopped, kicked off your sandals and rolled your jeans up to your knees. I saw that your toenails were painted bright red and your feet were slim and tanned.

'Come on,' you said. 'Let's go for a paddle. The water is still freezing but it is nice.'

I hesitated. I hated my feet. I hated the way my hammer-toes curled under, the way the skin looked white and sickly from being hidden away in shoes. But you held out a hand and said, 'Let's go, Miriam. You need to hear all the gossip before you meet the others.' You lowered your voice, pretending to be serious. 'I need to tell you who is going out together, who wants to be going out together, and who you need to run a mile from. We are going to have great fun, you and me.'

And then I did not care. I did not care about my feet, or my clothes, or my fears about being away from home. Instead, I felt the surprising thrill of friendship. Something fluttered inside me, like the wings of a small bird. You liked me, I could tell, and I felt myself grow that day. I felt myself turn towards the sun. Right at that moment, I began to be a different person. As we splashed our way into the sea, I thought of the girls at school, the way they sniggered that my name was really 'Primiam', not Miriam. I thought of the way they gave me a hard time because I was tall and skinny, not in a stylish way. I thought of the way I used to iron my long hair at home when Mother wasn't looking. But I could never tame the black waves that seemed to bounce back again. And now, suddenly none of that mattered so much.

I confided in you that afternoon. You smiled when I told you that my mother didn't believe in hairdressers. And you laughed when I told you how every two months she took the scissors to all of us. Derek protested the loudest, stamping out of the kitchen and up the stairs.

'No, Ma!' he would shout. 'I don't want to look like a bowl.' But she always caught him.

You listened and you nodded and you understood. I remember wondering how this could be. I had left all that was familiar behind me, yet now I had the strangest feeling that I had come home.

★

Were the days that followed golden and blue and perfect? Yes they were. I can remember no rain. Even then, the unusual weather made those endless weeks seem significant. It was no normal Irish summer. It was not filled with the damp sand and sticky towels of childhood holidays.

Instead, everything was bright, like our friendship and like all of the good things that were to come.

Chapter Two

I was surprised when Dad announced that he had found me a summer job. I had been told by Mother over and over that she simply could not spare me. Dad would nod each time he heard it, as if it were a piece of old wisdom. I understood only later that finding me this job was, in fact, an act of bravery on his part. It had little, if anything, to do with me.

There were five of us 'children'. Michael was the eldest and the quietest and I was next in line. There was barely a year between us. Then came Derek, the mouthy one, followed quickly by Joey and Bernard, who was only ever called Barney. Twin boys can take up an awful lot of space. And so it was with those two. They were eleven that year, the year I met you. I spent my entire life either waiting for the bathroom to be free, or picking up after both of them. Michael and Derek were not too bad, but Mother expected no help from any of them. Only from me.

I remember the way she glared at Dad when he told her about the summer job on a freezing February evening. 'Do you not think I have enough to do?' she demanded. 'You know I cannot spare Miriam for a full three months. What were you thinking?'

I was thinking about space, freedom, privacy. I tried to hide the great jolt of delight I felt as I watched Dad standing there. He had his hands in his pockets, and his pipe stuck firmly in the corner of his mouth. I had learned not to cross him when he clenched his teeth like that. I couldn't believe that Mother never had.

He turned away as the kitchen was filled with a loud, ticking silence. He settled himself into the armchair that sat in front of the fire. That chair was the only warm spot in the house. He rattled his newspaper. 'Extra money will come in handy,' he said. His tone was curt. 'As you keep reminding me.' He did not look up again.

Mother turned away slowly, back towards the sink. I slid out into the hallway and up the stairs to my room. When I came back, maybe an hour later, they were both still there, almost exactly as I had left them.

'Tell your father his tea is ready,' Mother said, wiping her hands on her apron.

★

You and I got back from the beach around three that afternoon. You sat on the top bunk in our room, legs dangling over the side. You swung them back and forth as I unpacked. I remember asking you about your family.

'Three sisters,' you said.

I was instantly jealous. Sisters!

'Audrey is the eldest and I am next. June is a year younger than me, and wee Megan is only ten. Mum says we spoil her rotten.'

As I listened, I was filled with a guilty longing to be part of your family. To have a mother who was so much younger and more glamorous than mine. To have a home that was full of good fun. To have a household not always short of money.

'I will take you there someday,' you said. 'Mum says that our door is wide open. There is always room for one more.'

'I would love that,' I said. 'Can we really go?'

You laughed at that. 'Of course we can! Really, really.'

I could see our future then, all mapped out before us. Friends for life. Me, you, maybe even your three sisters. That day, I wanted everything that seemed to fill that small room with promise. I can see it all. The dim, cramped space, the curtains that did not quite meet in the middle, the shabby furniture.

But to me, it was the bright, beating heart of the new life that you were offering me. The new life that was about to become mine.

*

Later that first day, I met Patricia. She was the older woman whose job it was to manage all the summer temps. Her dyed black hair was scraped back into a solid bun at the back of her neck. Her bright eyes missed nothing.

'So,' she said, lighting up a cigarette. She looked at me from behind a haze of smoke. We used to titter at the way she often had two fags going at the same time. Do you remember? One dangling from the corner of her mouth, the smoke making her scrunch up her right eye. She would already have at least one other fag lit, but she always forgot where she had put it. Sometimes it was in an ashtray on the sink where she did the washing-up, sometimes it was on the edge of the table. There were small burn marks everywhere. The lads used to nick the fags from the ashtray on their way out the back door to the boys' prefabs. I am sure she knew. But if she did, she never said.

'You are Miriam, then.'

I nodded.

'I am Patricia. You come to me if you have questions about anything, anything at all. Don't go bothering the managers, do you hear? They have enough to do.' She flipped through the pages of a hardback notebook. She did not even look up, so I didn't bother replying. 'I have you in with Marie-Claire.' She looked at me. 'You start at breakfast in the morning. Monica is in charge of the dining room and she will train you in. You follow her for a few days, just do what she does. For your first day, meet her here at six. Breakfast starts at seven.'

I nodded again. 'Okay.'

Patricia ground her cigarette butt into the plate in front of her. 'She will sort you out with a uniform and shoes. Have you ever waitressed before?'

I wondered if waiting on four boys and two adults counted. 'Not really,' I said.

'Does not matter. You will learn the ropes soon enough. Do as you are told, don't answer back and be polite to the guests. Oh, and try not to scald them.' She laughed at her own joke. We heard later about the waiter who had tripped and poured a whole pot of tea into the lap of an old man. Luckily, he had been waiting around for so long that the tea was almost cold. But it became one of the many cautionary tales of that summer.

I believed whatever I was told. You did not. You said you would keep me right.

★

'How did it go?' you asked the next morning, when the first wave of guests were finished breakfast. I had done what I was told, but I found the whole thing difficult. How was I supposed to remember so many things at once? Seven tables, twenty-eight strangers, all with different needs and wants. Bacon, egg and sausage. Bacon and sausage with no egg. Bacon with beans and mushrooms. Sausages with mushrooms and tomatoes. The variations felt endless. I wondered how Monica did it, how all the girls did it. We each had to work seven tables, but Monica made it look easy, striding up and down the dining room, all five-foot-nothing of her. The guests loved her. I could see the women respond to her smile. I watched the men watching her. The dip and swing of her hips, the easy tempo of her walk.

'My feet are killing me,' I said. 'I cannot wait until the shift is over.'

You smiled. 'Better not be too tired for tonight. Don't forget there is a live music session down in Lacey's.'

I'd never been to a pub. But that didn't seem the right time to tell you. Besides, I was still full of stress from the morning. It was bubbling away inside me.

'Focus on each guest when they are ordering,' Monica had told me. 'It helps to remember what they asked for. Match the face with the breakfast. Do not laugh! I'm serious. And do not worry, you will get used to it. They never change what they order, so you only have to learn it once.'

Once every fourteen days, she meant. The entire hotel population changed every two weeks. After the first day or so, I learned that this was not a hotel, not in any real sense. This was a holiday camp, open only for the summer. The guests came from the north of England. They were hard-working, hard-drinking mill workers and miners.

The Irish owner had made a business out of their needs. He had spotted a gap and set about filling it. He brought a dozen or so of the more experienced staff with him each season as managers, taking them from one of the pubs he owned. The rest of the staff was made up of students. I heard some of the older ones grumble from time to time about 'cheap labour' and I didn't understand. I thought I was earning a fortune. The owner was definitely earning a fortune. Every fortnight, the huge coaches would deliver two hundred elderly couples to the airport and replace them with two hundred others. They came year after year, lured by familiar food, a familiar language. Enticed by the prospect of days and half-days spent in places they already knew on organised tours with packed lunches. An 'all-in' holiday before such things became normal. 'We know where we stand, lass,' one of the older guests had told me. His blue eyes were still sharp and lively. 'All paid for up front, nothing to worry about. All I need is a couple of quid for a few pints and I'm right as rain.'

I used to see them at six in the morning, on my way to the dining room to lay the tables. I would watch them shuffle down the corridor in their dressing gowns. All men at that hour. They would be sent off by their wives to fetch their morning tea.

We used to laugh at them. 'The Straw People', you called them. And that is how they looked. Frail, dry, stuffed into tartan dressing gowns, stick-thin shins and ankles poking down into carpet slippers. It was as though they had no form of their own, as though the tartan gowns and belts were all that was keeping them upright. You never got to like them. But I grew to love their humour, their strong and quiet ways, their generosity. They were the best tippers I have ever known.

You used to tease the men. And they responded, of course they did. Being flirted with by a pretty girl did not happen to them often. There was sometimes an edge to your teasing, a less-kind undertow that they never got. Or maybe this is just me, with all the wisdom of hindsight.

'Look at them,' you once said, nudging me towards an old man and his wife who made their slow and painful way towards the café. 'Wouldn't you just hate to end up like that?'

Chapter Three

It was Tony, the bar manager, who told us about the overtime. It was almost the end of my first week and I was beginning to feel that things were becoming less strange. You and I were sitting in the staff kitchen, lingering over cups of tea long after the others had gone. We had finished our sandwiches and had a couple of hours to kill. Patricia was at one end of the room, finishing the washing-up, throwing us impatient glances from time to time.

'We will wash the cups, Patricia,' I said. 'Don't worry. We won't leave a mess.'

'Will you wipe down the table as well and put the cloths into the washing machine?' She looked at us out of her one open eye, her cloud of smoke shot through by a beam of sunlight. Through the huge window, I could see the ribbon of holiday-makers on their way down the hill towards the sand below us. There were no trips on Mondays, so our guests had to fend for themselves, something they never liked doing. They looked like a slow crocodile that had wandered off from a Chinese carnival. They carried parasols, windbreakers, folding chairs, picnic baskets in shades of red, yellow, blue and orange. The colours shone in the light.

I turned back to Patricia. The old people's parade to the beach had suddenly made me sad. 'Yes,' I said. 'We will. We will do a proper clean-up. Promise.'

'Right so,' she said, although her tone was reluctant. I do not know whether she wanted to be asked to join us, or whether she did not trust us. Either way, we were keen to get rid of her. She took off her apron slowly, put her cigarettes and lighter into her jacket pocket and made her way out the back door. She almost collided with Tony, who was on his way in.

'Afternoon, ladies,' he said. He nodded to Patricia. Even then, I remember being struck by how he did not seem to see her. It was as if she was just some random woman on her way out the door. Patricia looked back at us over one shoulder before she closed the door softly behind her.

Tony poured himself tea and sat down with us. He sat beside me, on the long bench that ran the entire length of the table. He sat facing you.

'Hi, Tony,' you said. 'How are you?' You took your packet of ten Carroll's out of your uniform pocket and Tony patted his shirt all over, in a comical rush to find a lighter.

'Sorry,' he said, 'seem to have left my fags and matches behind.'

28

You offered him one, but he refused. This ritual had begun to fascinate me. You could smoke anyone's cigarettes as long as you paid them back quickly. There were dark mutterings among the staff about those who smoked only 'O.P.s'. At first, I thought it was a brand I had not heard of. You let me think that for a while, and then you took pity on me. 'It means 'other people's'. Other people's cigarettes, because you are too tight to buy your own. Get it?' I learned that those who smoked only 'O.P.s' were the lowest of the low.

You smiled at Tony, lit your own cigarette and inhaled deeply. I tried to copy your elegant movements, once I started smoking myself. But I never quite got it. Years later, the first time that I saw Humphrey Bogart light Lauren Bacall's cigarette, I instantly thought of you. That day, with Tony sitting beside me, I became frozen by his presence. I could feel my cheeks burning. And my heart was hammering so hard that I thought you must have heard it, too.

'Now, isn't this lucky,' he said, 'finding you two here like this. I've been wanting to ask you something.'

'What is it?' You blew a thin stream of blue smoke towards the ceiling, still holding Tony's gaze. Then your eyes flickered towards mine, and I think in that moment you knew. I was just grateful that Tony wasn't looking at me, that you kept the conversation going and expected nothing from me.

'We have a big night tomorrow,' Tony said. He spoke quickly and I could hear the appeal in his voice. 'It is our talent show and we always get a lot of the locals in for it. I need extra floor staff, people with a bit of waiting experience. Would you be interested? Cash in hand, and the tips are your own business.'

You looked at me. All I could think of was Tony's arm beside mine on the table, and the dark hair on his wrists where it curled under his shirt cuff. I wanted to touch him so badly that I hardly heard your question. Just my name. And then Tony turned to look at me, his eyes bright blue, and I knew that something was finally expected of me.

'Um,' I remember saying. And then, as though I had just decided upon something, I said, 'Sure, why not? We aren't doing anything, are we?' I looked over at you, carefully not looking at Tony. Out of the corner of my eye, I saw that he drained his cup and heard him set it gently back on the saucer.

'No,' you said. 'We have a couple of things planned, but nothing that can't wait. What time would you want us, Tony?'

He stood up, stepping lightly over the bench. 'Say seven,' he said. 'Gerry will sort you out with a float. He will give you the heads-up on a couple of the local lads that you need to watch out for. And I will be there, if there's anything you need to ask.'

'Okay,' you said. 'See you then.'

'Yes,' I said. 'See you tomorrow.' The words sounded strangled, even to my ears.

And I suppose that became one of our defining moments. One of those times that are so clear looking back, but at the time are surprising, like a missed step or a breaking glass. You had to have seen how I felt. How hopelessly, carelessly, I had lost my heart.

But you stood up, gathering the cups and saucers and said, 'Right, let's get these washed up. I wonder what the talent show will be like?'

★

That night, we went to Lacey's. It was packed with people. The three pubs in the village were always jammed during the summer. The population grew to at least ten times its normal size, but not because of the hotel. The guests left the grounds only on Mondays, when they had to provide their own entertainment, but rarely after that. Besides, the owner made sure that none of his bar business went local. He kept his customers loyal with sandwiches and cocktail sausages at midnight and cheaper pints. He also had nightly entertainment that went from the talent shows to a steady stream of unknown, tired comedians already past their sell-by date.

Back then, the village was filled with bed and breakfasts, holiday cottages and caravan sites. Some of the farmers also gave over the odd field or two to campers if the weather was fine. In those days, nobody worried much about providing facilities. If you wanted to stay in a tent, then your bathroom stretched from the sea on one side to the fields that covered the North County on the other. I went back there once, about twenty years ago. It was on one of those grey winter days when curiosity had made me even more restless than usual.

Our harbour was empty. There was no sign of the fat seals that used to make the children from the nearby cottages scream with delight. The sea lapped at the wall in small swells. Along the waterline, the wall was green with seaweed, and I could see the oily scum of spilt diesel everywhere.

The hotel was long gone. The site was levelled, as though we had never been there. I had known that anyway. I had followed its changing fortunes, down through the years. What I did not know was that the pubs were also closed, as well as the local post office that used to double as a basic grocery store for the summer months.

We used to buy ice cream there. Then we would sit on the harbour wall, swinging our legs, watching the people go by. We would see romances begin to blossom among the hotel staff. We'd

watch as they ignited, then faltered, and
finally fizzled out. I already knew that
you had an antenna when it came to the
chemistry between people.

Anyway, Mrs Patton, the post-
mistress, used to stock milk and bread
in her little shop, and the odd packet of
cooked ham. She sold tomatoes, too,
from the crop that came in locally each
year. Baskets and baskets of North
County Dublin tomatoes with their
shiny flesh, their glorious greenness,
their stalks that smelt of cat piss. Real
tomatoes. I can still taste them. Mrs
Patton's fame, though, lay in the pots of
tea she sold for the holiday-makers'
picnics. That summer, our summer, she
had also bought one of those silver
machines that made soft, creamy swirls
of ice cream.

Mrs Patton was a smart lady. While
the mothers waited in line for their pots
of tea, the kids had time to look at the
ice cream machine in the corner, with

its giant ad for Flakes and 99s. Those mothers didn't stand a chance. Mrs Patton must have done well that season. Warm summers were rare even then. And while the post office was no longer open thirty years after we'd been there, it still had its signs outside. It still looked the same as it used to do. But the closed and shuttered pubs were far from what they once had been.

Just for a moment on that winter afternoon, I hesitated. I came close to walking back to the car, driving home, and forgetting that I had ever had a reason to go back there. Then curiosity drove me forward again. I crossed the muddy field to Lacey's to find that small window at the back, close to where we used to sit. It had escaped the attention of local vandals. Its murky pane of glass was still there.

I climbed onto a plastic crate and tried to peer inside. I thought I saw the shadowy outline of the oak bar, but I could not be sure. The garden was completely overgrown, the wooden barrels were rotting. The old fence was propped up here and there in a half-hearted attempt to keep out animals, or vagrants, or local youths.

That first night we had in Lacey's is burned into my memory. Not only had I never been to a pub before, I had never been at a live music session either. As we entered, the noise was deafening. Even the heat felt like noise. Drinkers had spilled out into the garden where barrels and bottle crates were being used as tables and chairs.

The evening was still bright. Up the hill to our right was the fun fair. I could see the swing boats with their swirls of yellow and red and orange. I could hear the echo of the fairground music being carried towards us on the evening breeze. I remember the yells of the children, each daring the other to go higher and higher, just as you and I did a couple of times that summer. The beach below us was scattered with groups of people, some wandering, some walking purposefully along its curving length. Children ran at the waves, dogs chased each other. Even at the time, the sights and sounds of that summer village filled me with longing for a childhood that had never been mine.

'What are you having?' you shouted.

I jumped. 'What?'

You rolled your eyes and laughed at me. 'To drink!' You moved closer and the pub's noise lessened.

'Oh, I do not know. What are you having?'

I saw you hesitate. 'Have you taken a drink before?'

I was about to lie until I saw the look you gave me. 'No,' I admitted.

'Okay,' you said. 'I will get you a vodka and orange. But you stop when I say so, all right?'

I nodded happily. I trusted you. 'All right,' I said. I could not stop grinning.

I was filled with optimism. The whole world seemed to be full of new and exciting experiences. In your presence, I felt that I hardly remembered the cold grey rooms of my parents' house.

Then the music started. There had been no music in my home. The radio was turned on for the news, the Angelus and sometimes Sunday mass at Christmas and Easter. Television was only for those programmes that were 'educational'. Mother did not believe in entertainment. Sometimes, on St Patrick's Day, traditional music would fill the kitchen for those slow afternoon hours after the parade. But that music was nothing like this.

Two fiddlers, a *bodhrán* player and a man with a squeeze box were sitting around a small table in the middle of the room. Nobody crowded them. Nobody came up to them as they made their music. Bar staff placed pints in front of them from time to time and then withdrew. The energy of their playing made the air around us electric. It fuelled the tapping feet, the clapping hands, the lively conversation that their instruments seemed to be having with each other.

My response was so unexpected, so surprising, that it took me some time to name it for what it was. I was confused by my own tears.

Later, a shy young boy with a set of pipes pulled his chair into the centre of the room. The other musicians carried their table back into the shadows, where they sat and listened. I don't think that the boy could have been more than fourteen. The same age as Derek and a whole two years younger than me. I suddenly missed my brother, his cheeky face and how he was unable to keep his head down when Mother raged. 'I can't help it,' he used to say to me. 'I can't let her get away with everything.'

As this young boy set up his pipes, the whole pub went silent, waiting for him to begin. When he played, his clear, emotional tunes thrilled me. It felt as though something inside me had taken flight. Even now, I can still feel the beat of the music in the soles of my feet. I can feel the glow that warmed my blood as I sipped the drinks you got at the bar. And I can still recall that feeling that was becoming familiar to me. A sense of life beginning at last, that somehow, my own story was just about to start.

Later, back in our room when my tongue was loosened by four vodkas and orange, I tried to talk to you about Tony. But you yawned and turned over, switching out the light. 'Tomorrow, Miriam,' you said. 'Let's talk about it tomorrow.'

But tomorrow came and went and you never mentioned Tony. Some new instinct made me hold my tongue.

It took the intimacy of our adventure together a few weeks later to give me the courage to try again.

Chapter Four

You took the bus home with me the next week. It was my day off and you had just finished your stint working in reception. The next day, we would be working together in the dining room. I would be the one showing you the ropes for a change. Even after just two weeks, I was getting much better. I had mastered the breakfast orders much faster than I had expected. Lunch and dinner offered the guests a limited choice, so my working day got easier and easier. 'People do not want to make decisions on their holidays,' Monica had told me. 'At least, these people don't. Good food, plenty of it, and every night spent in the bar.'

I suppose I was happy that I was able to do things, happy that Monica and others had called me 'bright'. It made me think that Dad was right, after all. Maybe I did deserve more than the life that Mother had planned for me.

Anyway, I had just got paid for my first two weeks and I was excited to show off at home, to deliver my pay in person. I needed Mother to see what I could do. When I rang her from the phone box in the village, she seemed almost pleased to hear from me. 'It is eleven pounds a week, Mam, into my hand. And there's a bonus of two pounds a week at the end, if I stay for the whole season.'

When we got off the bus, my brother Michael was there. Mother must have told him what time we were arriving. I saw the way he looked at you. I do not know why, but up until that moment, I

had never thought of Michael as a man.
He was still a boy, with a boy's annoying
habits. But that morning, I saw his eyes
widen. I watched as a deep flush crept
up his cheek. In that moment, my
brother changed for me. I think he
changed for himself, too.

You were charming to my parents.
My father took to you at once, of
course. He lingered over his lunch,
staying at the table longer than normal.
I think he would have stayed for the
afternoon if Mother's silent disapproval
had not been so obvious. She was much
more wary of you, which was just as I
would have expected. But by the time
we left that afternoon, her smile was
almost warm.

Earlier, upstairs on our own, I had
handed Mother my pay. She kissed my
forehead. It was a dry, papery kiss. I
could not hide my eagerness, how
newly grown-up I felt. 'It will help with
the schoolbooks and things, won't it?'

She looked at me then, and I could not read her expression. She seemed to be struggling with something. 'Yes,' she said. 'It certainly will.' When I was leaving, she almost hugged me. 'You are a good girl,' she said. 'A good girl.' And she slipped four ten-shilling notes into my hand. I do not think either Michael or Derek noticed. They had eyes only for you.

I felt astonishment, followed by a hot surge of guilt. I looked down to where my mother's hand still rested on my forearm. I wanted to say something, but I could not. I could not tell her about all the overtime we had been working. That other money was mine. For the first time ever, I could use it any way I liked. But the sight of my mother's crooked knuckles made me feel ashamed. I hugged her back quickly, glad that Dad was no longer there to see. I would never have been able to fool him.

After that visit, Michael took the bus from Dublin to see us two or three times that summer. He really only came to see you. After you went away sometime around the beginning of August, I watched his misery grow.

But by then, everything had changed anyway.

★

One night earlier that year, maybe sometime in March, I overheard my parents' angry voices in the kitchen. Sound travelled in that house. It seeped through floorboards and closed doors. It snaked down corridors, filtered its way through thin walls. It seemed to follow the same route as cold air that was always in our household. My parents were arguing about me.

'She is old enough,' I heard. 'She has got a good Inter Cert behind her. What is wrong with a commercial course?'

I had to strain a little to hear Dad's reply. It was one of his tactics. The more shrill Mother became, the more softly he spoke. 'She is not doing a commercial course. Miriam is bright, she deserves better.'

Mother must have lowered her voice, too, because all I heard next was 'Four boys.'

Dad's reply was sudden and sharp. He said, loudly, that he did not need to be reminded of his duty to his children and how dare she speak to him like that.

I held my breath and wondered how soon I would be able to get out of there for good. To leave them all behind and begin living the life that I knew was out there, somewhere, waiting for me.

*

Our bar nights with Tony became regular events during the next few weeks. There was no shortage of overtime and I quickly learned that a smile and a kind word kept the tips coming. On that first night, as agreed, we arrived at seven. Gerry, the assistant manager, was already there, setting out ashtrays, moving chairs, making space around the circular tables. There were even candles that night. Fat white ones on every table, along with a small vase with one red paper flower.

'Right, girls,' he said. 'Follow me.'

We each got trays and a pint glass that contained a 'float'. I had not understood the word when Tony said it, but I kept quiet.

'Take the orders at the table and pay for the drinks at the bar with your float,' Gerry said. 'Then the guests pay you.' I could see how bored you looked. You had done this before. Besides, you did not like Gerry. He was small and round and balding. I do not believe you even saw him. 'You are each getting five quid in change,' Gerry went on, wiping his sweaty forehead. 'Keep it safe, in the glass. You have to give it back at the end of the night. Any mistakes, you make up the cash from your tips. Any questions?' The evening began with a roar of activity. Hundreds of people spilling into the room as soon as Tony opened the doors. I was glad of the chance to watch him. I loved how his dark hair fell to just below his shirt collar and the easy way he moved about the room. I glanced in his direction every chance I got. Every so often, he caught my eye and smiled. I could feel myself blush every time.

It took a few minutes for the guests to settle. Everyone wanted to be near the stage to watch the talent show. I remember that there was some pushing and shoving. Some of the guests seemed to find a new and startling strength in order to get what they wanted. There was no shuffling of slippers that night.

The orders for drinks began at once. It became a matter of pride to be the fastest on my feet. There were seven girls and seven boys on that night. We never stopped. My apron pocket became heavy with coins. The thrill of that. The weight of the tips, the money that was all mine. All earned for nothing other than being nice.

You had the measure of everyone. Take Eddie, the junior barman, for example, and what happened on that first night. You prodded me, even before the evening's work had begun, and whispered that 'the wee brat' was not to be trusted. From you, I learned that people are not always as they seem. Towards the end of the night, I saw you leaning on the bar, talking to Eddie. I could see at once that something was wrong. As I got closer, I could hear you arguing.

'I am not stupid,' you said. 'I know exactly what you have been doing. You had better put it right.'

I saw him shrug, his eyes on the tap as he pulled a pint of Guinness. Finally, he dug in his pocket and slammed some coins on the counter in front of you. He never spoke, never once looked at you.

I caught you as you turned away. Your eyes were blazing, your cheeks flushed.

'What is wrong?' I asked.

'That wee bastard short-changed me not once but twice. You watch yourself. I think he's been doing it all night.'

I can still remember the shock. The boldness of it left me without words. I had never thought that one of us might try to cheat the other. We all lived cheek by jowl. We ate together, went to the beach together. We met each other constantly, between shifts in the hotel or in one of the village pubs. How could Eddie do that? I quickly counted my float. I was a full two pounds short. I tasted anger. It was an ashy, gritty taste that filled my mouth. But I had not caught him in the act like you had. I had no evidence.

'I am telling Tony,' you said, later. 'He should not be allowed to get away with it.'

I can still feel the stab of jealousy that made me catch my breath. I had been too slow, too stupid to catch on.

If I had been smarter, I would have been the one with a reason to talk to Tony. To seek him out. To make him see me.

★

It was 1973. Exactly forty years ago this summer. There are so many things now that I forget. So few things that stand out with any clarity. But it seems that the further away I get from that time, the sharper my memory becomes.

Chapter Five

Sometime near the end of June, you woke me early one morning, a good hour before our usual rising time. I had gone to bed an hour or two before you the previous night. I felt run-down after a double shift and two nights of overtime. All those hours on my feet. You never seemed to run out of energy. You were always able to stay behind with the others after cleaning up, have a couple of drinks, get to bed by two and be up again for five-thirty. I didn't understand it.

Besides, I was suffering. I found it hard to be in Tony's company and not be noticed by him. To be fair, he did not seem to notice any of us. He was about five years older than most of the students who worked there. These summers were no longer new to him. I remember thinking that he had a whole other city life that he must be missing. The thought depressed me that night in particular. I went to bed and tried to blot it out.

The following morning, I became aware of someone urgently shaking my shoulder. For one dream-filled moment, I thought I was at home again, in my own bedroom. I struggled against a surge of disappointment.

'Miriam, wake up.'

And then I knew it was you. I knew that I was still here, still in that other life that was quickly becoming mine. I became alert at once. 'What? What's wrong? Have we slept it out?'

You leaned over the upper bunk, your hair a bright sheen against the blue curtains. 'Listen to me,' you said. Your face was in shadow but I could feel your excitement. 'I. Have. A. Plan.'

'A plan for what?'

You dropped from your bunk to the floor, pulling across the curtains that couldn't keep the light out anyway. 'A road trip,' you said. Your voice filled with delight. 'You and me. Three, maybe four days.'

I didn't get it. 'A what trip?'

'A road trip! Just us girls together! Let's drive across the country to, I do not know, Galway maybe. Or Cork. Somewhere we have never been! Adventure, Miriam! Let's have an adventure!' I had never had an adventure before. This job was as close as I had ever come to an adventure. I looked at you, at the excitement on your face, the way your eyes shone. I struggled to sit up and pushed the blankets back. 'When? And how will we get there?'

You laughed and twirled in the half-light, your nightgown clinging to your curves as you did a neat spin, and a neater bow. 'By car, of course!' You dipped your face closer to mine and winked.

'Whose car? Who will drive?' You had such energy. I began to feel once again the way I had felt in Lacey's pub when the music had begun, when happiness flooded my veins. Feelings bubbled beneath my surface. Things like delight, a sense of possibility, a whole world of freedom.

'Gerry's car, of course. I will drive!'

I was not sure of what I had heard. And I did not know you could drive. I must have looked completely blank.

'Gerry's,' you said again. 'You know, the wee baldy guy.'

'I know who Gerry is,' I said. 'I just do not understand how we have got his car.'

'Does it matter?' you asked.

I struggled to find an answer. I felt I was failing some sort of test.

'If you must know, Gerry's stuck here for the next three weeks. Barry cancelled his leave. One of the relief managers is sick. So . . .' and you twirled again, 'I asked him last night if we could borrow his car and he said yes.'

Your face was filled with pride. I finally understood what it was that you were offering me. 'A whole three or four days away from here? On our own?' I quickly calculated how much money I had saved. I could feel my breath getting faster.

You nodded. 'Yes. We have at least two days off coming to us anyway. We can swap shifts with the other girls for the third one and then next week we are out of here!'

'We can do more overtime in the bar,' I said. 'I earned three quid in tips last night. They are getting to know us. We will have loads!' I was almost shouting. Finally, this was what being an adult was like. I had to answer to nobody, I could learn to fly.

'Come on,' you said. 'Let's get washed and dressed. I will show you the car before breakfast.'

★

I think it was the first time I ever lied on purpose. I had fibbed before, of course, and told white lies from time to time. Though I had never set out to deceive.

Mother was disappointed. 'Can you send the money by postal order if you cannot get home?' she said. 'Joey and Barney need new shoes this week. They are growing out of everything.' She said it like a complaint, as though the twins had done it to annoy her.

'The post office is closed,' I lied. I was very glad that she could not see my face. I prayed that Dad would not come to the hotel that week or the next for one of his visits. He would find me out at once.

'Mrs Patton is on holidays until the end of next week. I will send the money as soon as I can.' I had already figured out how many double shifts I would need to work to make up the loss. But right now, all I wanted to buy was time. And right now, for the first time in all my sixteen years, I was feeling reckless. Part of me did not care what my father or mother found out. If it all went to plan, my road trip would be over by the time they did. At that moment, it seemed that they were both very far away from me, as if some thread between us had been cut. That new distance suddenly felt right.

'Well, that will have to do, I suppose.'

I could hear her sigh. A breath of disappointment that for once didn't bother me. I was thrilled. I felt I had escaped some terrible fate.

'Have to go, Mam,' I said. 'I am on duty in half an hour.'

Another lie. It was becoming easier. It was my afternoon off and I was

heading to the beach with you, Gary,
Megan and Tom.

★

The rest of that week passed in a fever
of waiting. Each day, we would sit in the
car for half an hour and plan our trip. I
say 'plan', but really we had no idea
where we wanted to go. 'We will follow
the first signpost,' was all you would
say. 'As long as it is not north.' The car
was low and white and tiny. It was a
Fiat 500 with shabby seats and an
overflowing ashtray. You drove around
the car park several times, until at last
we stopped lurching and stalling. You
guessed what I was thinking.

'I am just out of practice,' you said.
'Do not look at me like that.'

The following day, just after lunch,
you came to find me in the staff kitchen.
'Gerry's just told me I have to double
de-clutch,' you said. 'That is why we've
been stalling.'

I did not have a clue what that meant. I was just glad that I would no longer be thrown towards the windscreen every time you started the engine.

When Tuesday morning came, we whispered our final plans. We did not want to wake any of the others. We wanted no advice, no company for our departure. You had a large orange rucksack that just about fitted in the boot. We shared it. My suitcase was too embarrassing, too old-fashioned to be part of an adventure. We sat into the car and you handed me a soft tartan bag. 'Open it,' you said.

Inside was a Kodak Instamatic. 'You are the official adventure photographer,' you said, grinning. 'We can have evidence of everything we get up to!'

We left at five, dawn already creeping above the village roofs. We had pinched some stuff from the kitchen. Bread rolls, ham, cheese. You had even made a flask of coffee.

'Galway,' you said suddenly as we left the village streets behind. 'I have decided. Definitely Galway.'

I was too happy to care that I had no part in that decision. I rolled the passenger window down, kicked off my sandals and put my feet up on the dashboard. The air rushing through the open window was cool on my skin. I laughed out loud for no reason, for all sorts of reasons.

You turned and grinned at me. 'Here,' you said, tossing me your pack of cigarettes. 'Light us one.'

'Us?'

'Why not?' you said. 'Live a little!'

I lit both cigarettes at once, inhaling the way I'd seen Patricia do. I handed one to you. Strangely, I felt none of the discomfort I had expected. I did not cough, or splutter, or even go green. I knew you would have told me if I changed colour. I drew the smoke in deep, felt the top of my head ignite and my fingers begin to tingle.

You looked at me with a sideways glance.

'Well, well,' you said. 'Fancy that. Who would have thought wee Miriam would be a natural smoker?'

And so I was. I felt absurdly proud of that. I did not confess to feeling just a little bit sick. I was determined to perfect the skill. Holding the cigarette gave me confidence. I could pretend that my fingers were slender and elegant like yours, that my nails were not bitten and ugly. I could pretend that the smoke I inhaled helped me absorb some of your glamour.

Above everything, it was another escape. Like the music, like the vodkas and orange, like the buzz of waitressing – they all helped me pretend to be someone else.

★

We stopped in Athlone. The drive was a hard one. The road was single lane all the way. You swore like a trooper each time we became trapped behind a tractor. Your overtaking grew more reckless as we reached Athlone and I was glad to pull over.

'Welcome to the dead centre of Ireland,' I said. It was Dad's phrase, one of many that I had grown up with. He was surprisingly witty, my father.

I was taken aback at your sudden laugh. 'That is good,' you said. 'That is funny. I will remember that.' You looked around us and shook your head. 'Jesus. Dead is right. What a dump, even in the sunshine.'

I took photographs of everything. I wanted to remember every minute, even the grey ones.

We needed petrol. I also needed to uncurl myself from the cramped front seat. We bought chocolate and sat in a side street that led to a grey housing estate. After the chocolate, we drank coffee from the flask and smoked. Just as we were about to leave, you leapt out of the car, saying 'I almost forgot!' You ran around to the boot and began rooting in your rucksack. I had no idea what you were looking for. At that point, I had just discovered that while the passenger window might have opened easily, it now stubbornly refused to close again.

'Look!' you said. 'Imagine forgetting these!'

'These' were a dozen or so cassettes, some in their hard plastic cases, some not. You tumbled them into my lap. 'Find Neil Young,' you said. 'It is a tape called *Harvest*. He is just brilliant, so he is.' When I found the right cassette, it had a thin brown ribbon of tape escaping, curling away into a shiny 'S' in my lap. I had no idea what to do with it.

'Here,' you said, and handed me a biro. You showed me how to rewind the tape into its cover, twisting it patiently back into place.

'Will it still work?' I did not think it would.

You pointed to the cassette player. 'Give it a go.'

At first, nothing happened.

'Press rewind,' you said. 'Gerry said the tape deck was definitely working. Give it another go.'

I pressed play. The music started at once.

'Turn it up!' you said. 'Turn it right up!'

Sound filled the car. It was as if the tiny Fiat became a giant loudspeaker. I felt as though we were inside the music, floating somewhere between worlds. You sang along with gusto to the first two tracks. To be honest, I wanted you to stop. This was music of another kind, one I hadn't heard before. I wanted to listen to Neil Young's strange, beautiful voice. You stopped singing then.

'Listen,' you said. 'I will shut up and you just listen. I know all these tracks off by heart since last year. I wish it was my first time to hear them.'

Just like that night in Lacey's, the music began to stir something inside me. I felt as though my head and heart were opening up. I felt that my old self was pouring outwards and upwards, and something new and exciting was taking root where I had once been. I followed the beats of 'Heart of Gold', listened to the lyrics and felt that I was hearing wisdom for the first time. I remember thinking that you were the 'heart of gold' that I had been looking for all my life. I had never realized that friendship could hold such power.

'This is amazing' I said. 'This music, this trip, this last month.' I stopped, not sure if I could say what I wanted to say next. I could feel my cheeks getting warmer, knew that tears were about to flow. 'I have never had a friend like you.'

You reached across and squeezed my hand. You murmured something, something that sounded like 'wee pet'.

Chapter Six

Later, much later, we found Father Griffith Road and with it, our bed and breakfast. We were glad to get out of the car, it had been three hours since Athlone, a few missed turns, a few confusing sets of directions. And we were starving. 'Let's wash and change,' you said, hauling the rucksack out of the boot. 'Then we are off on the town.' We rang the bell and stepped into a dim hallway that smelt of cabbage.

Our landlady, Mrs Doherty, was suspicious the minute she saw the orange rucksack. I thought at once of

Mother and her fear of hippies and jeans and people who took drugs. 'This is a lovely room, Mrs Doherty,' I lied, as she showed us upstairs. I ignored the look you gave me. The room was cheap, it was ugly, but it was ours and I badly needed to use the bathroom. There was a smell of damp in the air, only half-masked by the nasty, metallic scent of air freshener. I spotted the huge aerosol can in the corner. The flowery wallpaper was peeling and the yellow candlewick bedspreads had small baldy patches in several places. I remembered how I had got into trouble at home for picking at those strands when I was younger, and I wondered where Mrs Doherty's children were.

'Thank you,' I said, and smiled at her. To my surprise, she turned to leave. 'I will give you the keys when you are both ready,' she said. 'Just knock on the kitchen door before you go out.' And she made her way down the stairs, her back stiff with disapproval.

I was ready first and sat on the lower bunk, waiting for you. I had brought my book, one I had had very little chance to read since I started work at the hotel. It was called *The House on the Strand*. I can still remember how that story gripped me.

I had had to hide it at home, of course. There were no books in our house, unless you counted Butler's *Lives of the Saints*. I think there were twelve volumes. Green leather, a wedding present to my parents. Dad had signed my library application form with his usual warning, 'Do not tell your mother.' The library became my home. I went there after school as much as I could. I borrowed at least three books a week, every week, hiding them in a box of Christmas decorations. The week I met you was the third time I had borrowed *The House on the Strand*. I could not get enough of it. I loved the tale of a man being transported to another world, escaping his ordinary life. It is a book that

I re-read even now, from time to time. I still manage to lose myself in the story, almost as much as the first time I read it.

That evening in Galway, I don't know how long you had been looking at me. I just suddenly became aware of an odd, charged silence.

'Have you ever had a boyfriend?' you asked.

I must have blushed, or looked embarrassed, because you instantly said, 'Do not be upset, I am not being nosey. I am asking for a reason.'

'No,' I said. 'I never have.' I toyed with the pages of my book, feeling pain begin its slow beat somewhere underneath my heart.

You nodded. 'I know you have fallen for Tony,' you said. 'And I think you are cross with me because we have not talked about it.'

'No!' I said. 'I am not cross, it's just. . .' I trailed off, because I did not know what I was. But 'cross' did not enter into it. I could not have been cross with you.

'I think he's way too old for you,' you said. 'He's almost twenty-four.'

I felt my eyes fill. You came and sat beside me right away. 'He does not notice me, anyway,' I said. I wiped my eyes hurriedly. 'It does not matter. Let's forget about it. I am having a great time.'

You nodded. 'What about any of the others? Gary and Brian and Tom. Would you fancy any of them?'

I shook my head. But something occurred to me as I looked at you, all dressed up in your black Levi's and your gypsy blouse. My cotton skirt felt hopelessly old-fashioned and ugly. 'Will you come shopping with me?'

'What?' You seemed surprised, as if you had expected me to say something else.

'You know, shopping for clothes.'

'Here in Galway?'

'Yes. Tomorrow.' I was almost afraid to ask. I did not know what else you might have had planned for our adventure.

You shrugged. 'Sure. Why not?'

I was all eagerness then. 'I want jeans and tops and dresses and anything that is different from this.' I tugged at my skirt in disgust.

'Have you enough money?'

I grinned then. The world was brighter. 'I am loaded,' I said.

I gave only the briefest of thoughts to Joey and Barney and their new shoes, to Mother and her worries. To three days' time when all this would be over and we would be back in the real world again.

You pulled me to my feet. 'We will start first thing tomorrow morning. And,' here you tugged at my hair, 'you might want to get a haircut as well.'

I stopped you as you were about to leave the bedroom. 'Does he know?' I asked suddenly. 'Does Tony know?'

You hesitated, just for an instant. 'I think he probably does. We girls are not the best at hiding it.'

I was mortified. 'He probably thinks I'm stupid,' I said. I remember feeling real despair.

You took me by the shoulders and made me look at you.

'Listen to me,' you said. 'There are plenty of fish in the sea. The others would give their eye teeth to go out with you. Think about it. Maybe Tony's not the one for you.'

I nodded, biting my lip. I had no interest in those boys. They reminded me of my brothers. But I did not tell you that.

'Now come on,' you urged. 'Galway is waiting for us!'

★

We ate fish and chips with our fingers, just beside the Spanish Arch. It was the best fish and chips I have ever had.

And then we found a pub with music. This was not a difficult thing to do in Galway. Music is everywhere there, but your taste was spot-on. Not just any old music would do. You knew exactly what you wanted, just as you did with so many things. Boys flocked to where we sat that night, like moths to your flame. They posed with you, hanging around until you dismissed them. My photos show you and all of them laughing, red-eyed from the flash of the Instamatic.

As we walked home afterwards, a bit unsteady, I asked you, 'Have you got a boyfriend, then?'

You paused while you lit us both a cigarette, handed me one, and then started walking again. You seemed to be thinking over something. 'I have,' you said. 'His name is Matt.'

'What's he like?' I was eager for all the details, now that we were equals. Okay, I did not yet have a boyfriend, but our conversation had made me feel that I could have, if I wanted to. It gave me confidence. 'Is he a hunk?'

'Yes,' you said. 'He is surely.' You looked straight ahead, sending smoke signals out into the warm velvety night.

Vodka had made me brave. 'Where is he? Why isn't he with you?'

It may have been a trick of the street light, or this could be the wisdom of hindsight, but I saw something in your face change.

'It's complicated,' you said. 'But we will be together when we go back to university.'

I wanted to ask you more but I didn't.

*

We hit the shops in Galway city centre the following morning just as they were opening. You were a whirlwind. You brought me things to try on. You kept coming with pair after pair of jeans until I had the perfect fit. By noon, I had spent almost everything I had saved on jeans, tight tee-shirts, two maxi dresses that were in the summer sale, and a miniskirt. I was overjoyed. I did not have enough to pay the hairdresser, but you lent me money to keep me going.

I threw away my old homemade cotton skirts and dresses before we headed back. I left them behind me in the wardrobe of Mrs Doherty's bed and breakfast. I did not even hang them up, just left them in a crumpled heap on the shelf. It felt like shedding an old skin, in spite of the sense of betrayal that came with it.

On our way back to reality, we took a detour to Connemara. Women dressed in black walked the narrow roads, dark shawls covering their heads. Men looked at us with wariness as we drove by. Skinny children stood, silent and barefoot, as we passed. The harsh land glowed in the sunlight, the sea was a blinding blue and green.

We stopped in Carraroe and I used up a whole roll of film. Everything there was different from anything else I had ever seen. I had a sense of being fully awake, of being aware and alert and alive. Everything was possible now. Escape, love, university. All the things you had already found for yourself.

'Do we have to go back?' I asked. Suddenly, the thought of the Straw People and the hotel felt so limiting, like living with the sound turned down.

You laughed. 'We will do it again, before the summer is over. We will have another adventure like this one.'

'Promise?'

'I promise,' you said. 'Now turn up the music.'

★

The boys certainly noticed me. I got some wolfwhistles the night we returned and some compliments from the guests. Tony's eyebrows shot up when he saw the pair of us.

'Where have you two ladies been?' he asked. 'We have missed you.'

'We have been having an adventure,' you said.

Tony laughed. 'You both look as if you've been up to no good. Any chance of one of you working tonight?'

'Yes,' I said quickly.

'I think I will give tonight a miss,' you said. 'I'm a wee bit tired after all that driving. But put me down for tomorrow night.'

I worked all the hours God sent for the next four nights. By Tuesday, I had enough money to send home by postal order so that my mother would not suspect what I had been up to. Saturday was change-over day, and the guests at each of my seven tables had left me a tip of a pound. The generous standard was five shillings per person. I had been relying on that money, and I was relieved when I got it. I bid goodbye to all my guests as they left. I thanked them for their tips, and stood in the driveway waving until the coach taking them to the airport was out of sight.

I worked so hard that I hardly noticed Tony was not there. It just seemed that Gerry was always around instead, with Brian and Gary as his assistants. And then the shifts changed. They changed without warning and I was left confused.

Chapter Seven

It happened when I had gone home for my day off. You did not come with me. You said that you had got a letter from a friend at university, who was driving out to see you at the hotel. I was disappointed, and I knew that my brother Michael would be too. When I got home that day, I decided to tell him about Matt. I didn't think it was fair to let him hold out hope. Before I got the bus home, I carefully dressed in one of the skirts that my mother had made me. I had been smart enough not to throw out everything.

My brother met me at the bus stop, just as he had the time before. I knew by his face that I was not what he had been expecting. You were the main event, I was unimportant. On the walk home, he asked where you were. I could not bear how eager he was. He reminded me of myself. 'She has a boyfriend, Mike,' I said at last, and watched as his face coloured.

He had already come to see us at the hotel once, a couple of days before our adventure. He had taken the bus without being invited, and simply arrived, asking for me. Patricia had been kind to him and found me in the dining room to let me know he was there. I warned you to say nothing about our road trip. We took him to Walsh's pub at the far end of the village, where the hotel staff never went. It wasn't 'cool' enough. Although that is not the word we would have used back then.

I felt sorry for my brother that night. He spent the evening with us, listening to the music. He hung on everything you said, looking at you when you were not paying attention. I knew he was unhappy. Traditional music was not why he had made the trip to see us. You had been nice to him, but only in the way you would be nice to anyone's brother. Of course he was too young for you, he was too shy and ill at ease. I knew that. But hope is a cruel master.

'I will come and see you at the hotel, just one more time,' he said. 'She might change her mind.' I felt sorry for him all over again. His longing for you was so strong I could almost taste it. We had reached our front door by then and I could just see my mother's apron in the hall. I knew Michael and I would not get another chance to talk like this.

I shook my head. 'I don't think so,' I said. 'I am sorry, Mike. I thought it only fair to tell you.'

All of him seemed to fall inwards. He crumbled with disappointment.

'Thanks,' he said bitterly. He did take the bus one more time at the end of July. But as I said, things had already changed by then.

★

When I got back the following morning, Patricia was waiting for me. She called me to the table in the staff room where she always sat with her hardback notebook and ashtray.

'We have had some changes,' she said. 'A couple of the waiting staff have left.'

'Why?' I was surprised.

'Different reasons,' she said. I knew I would find out nothing else from her. I needed you and Nessa and Brian and Gary for that sort of gossip.

In the event, the gossip was not all that interesting. Family stuff. A birthday, a wedding, a sudden illness. That sort of thing. 'What it means for us is that we have to change the shifts. You will be working a couple of hours longer each time. But you will be paid time and a half, with a bonus for every five extra hours you work. It will be worth your while,' Patricia told me.

I did not argue, did not question her. What else would I be doing, anyway?

'I'm taking you off the floor for the next week, and you will work the café with Tom. He's a nice lad.'

I nodded. Tom was long and gangly, with a wicked sense of humour. I remembered what you had said about him fancying me. I thought it might be a bit of fun to work with him.

'I need you to help him out this afternoon. From now until the café closes at eight. He will train you in. You are quick and bright so you will have no problems.' She almost smiled at me as she lit a cigarette. 'And you can still do overtime in the bar at night if you want. I will talk to Gerry about a later start for you. You do not need to be there at seven.'

'Okay, that is fine.' I hung my bag over one shoulder. I pushed back my chair and stood up. 'Have you seen Marie-Claire?'

Patricia shook her head. She was staring at her cigarette. 'No. Not recently.'

'Have her shifts changed too?'

Patricia nodded. 'Yes. I'm sure she will tell you herself.'

I felt dismissed, as though I had misbehaved in some way. But Patricia was writing in her notebook, not looking at anything except the page in front of her.

I made my way up to our room to change. I spent the afternoon serving tea, coffee and fairy cakes to the Straw People.

★

This is where things start to become blurry, where the days start to lose their shape. With the change in shifts, you and I kept missing each other. We still went to the odd music session together in Lacey's, but our overtime nights in the bar never seemed to match up. You came to the room late, after I had gone to bed. My rising time was even earlier now. I had to prepare for the crowds of men in dressing gowns who came for their tea at dawn.

And I never went back to working the dining room. Patricia kept me on in the café, with Tom. I had been right. He was fun to work with, and I think the guests saw us as a kind of double act and were greatly entertained by us. Business had never been so good.

'It used to be the weak link,' Patricia told me. 'But you and Tom have turned the café around. You make the guests laugh. Mr Butler is really pleased with you. He even told your dad.'

I already knew that. Dad was proud of me. The fact that his daughter had turned out to be a success looked good for him too. I was happy for him, and also happy for myself. I was earning a fortune in tips. Even being generous to my mother with my postal orders, I had plenty of money left for myself. Plenty to put away for our next adventure, one I was sure was coming.

You went home to Donegal for a few days in July. Something to do with enrolling for university. I spent a lot of time at the beach with the others, lazing through the hot days, swimming and reading. I began to get used to the ache that was always beneath my heart. The pain of seeing Tony every day hurt, and it was made even worse by knowing he was out of my reach. Tom tried to woo me, he really did. Brian and Gary made a couple of tries, too. But I was not interested. I felt almost sorry for Tom. I understood the pain that I might be causing him, but there was no help for that.

Chapter Eight

Towards the end of July, something happened.

I was sitting in the staff kitchen one evening, just after eight o'clock. Tom and I had closed shop for the night. There was nobody else around, and it was the quiet hour that I loved. I would look out at the sea. At the small groups of people on the beach and the sky before a late sunset. I sat with my back against the wall, my feet up on the long bench. My cigarette was burning in the ashtray beside me. I was reading *Rebecca*. To my great delight, Patricia had told me about the cupboard where guests left books they had finished reading. It was a treasure trove. It made me see some of the Straw People in a new light.

And suddenly, Patricia was beside me.

'Miriam,' she said. 'Didn't expect to find you here. No overtime tonight?'

'No,' I said. 'I am a bit fed up with it, to be honest.'

'Is Marie-Claire not around?' Patricia walked over to the sink and put on the kettle. 'Cup of tea?'

'Tea would be great, thanks. No, I have not seen her today. We seem to keep missing each other.'

Patricia nodded. I noticed that her roots were showing. They were pale grey against the shiny black of her hair. I felt sorry for her, sorry that she was getting old.

I put my book on the table when she came over with the teapot. I reached across and took two mugs from the shelf.

'You are a great reader,' she said. 'Never caught the bug myself, I'm afraid.'

I smiled back. Then I waited. There was something about her that told me change was coming. And even though she did not have her notebook with her, I knew that she was about to change my working day again. I sat up and put my feet on the floor. I was prepared to argue with her. The days with Tom were easy and gentle and I did not want to be put back into the dining room or on the bar.

Patricia stirred her tea. 'Are things still going well in the café?' she asked. 'All okay with Tom?'

I nodded. 'Yes. It's all good.'

She looked at me. 'He's a lovely lad,' she said. 'And I think he has taken a shine to you.'

I felt annoyed, embarrassed and guilty. It was as if I owed Tom something that I wasn't giving because I had failed to fancy him, just because he fancied me.

'I know that is not where your heart lies,' Patricia went on. 'At least, it is not where you think it lies.' She sipped at her tea and then reached for her cigarettes.

I was speechless.

She offered me a cigarette. 'I am going to tell you something,' she said. 'And perhaps I should not. Perhaps it is none of my business. But I think you are a lovely girl and I have known your father for years.'

I think that at some deep-down level, I already knew what was coming. But I did not want to hear it. I raised my hand, fighting off the truth of whatever Patricia had started to say. But she would not stop.

'I do not want to see you made a fool of,' she said.

*

A little later on, that talk with Patricia made me wonder. Not at the time, of course. But afterwards. I remembered the way her face softened when she mentioned my father. I remembered her kindness to Michael, and to me. And I remember thinking that I hoped my father had once been tender with her.

God knows, he got little enough tenderness at home.

I didn't believe a word Patricia said, of course. At first I was angry, so angry that I stamped out of the staff kitchen and up the stairs to our room. I waited for you, but you never came. Finally, I took my shoulder bag and a jumper and made my way down to the beach. The sun was setting and all around me, the failing light made shadows. People seemed larger than life. Shapes shifted and changed towards menace. Even the collie dogs with their wagging tails seemed dangerous.

I went towards the fire. There was a beach party going on. It was the night before change over day. The new guests would not arrive until early the next morning. Around twenty of the hotel staff were sitting around. They were strumming guitars, drinking beer and singing songs. There were a few couples kissing , a few sleeping bags moving on the damp sand. Tom spotted me and called me over. His eyes were bright, too bright, and he was loud in a way that was not natural for him.

'Miriam,' he said, as though I had made all his wishes come true, just by arriving. He kissed me on the cheek. It was a long, wet kiss that made me angry all over again. I pulled away from him.

'Here she is,' I heard. I saw two girls I barely knew sitting close together and giggling. One was called Martha. 'Friendship is about sharing, isn't it?' Martha said loudly, waving her beer bottle in my direction. 'Caring and sharing. Sharing everything?'

'Yes,' her friend said. 'How come you don't do that for me?'

They burst into fits of laughter. I just stood there like the village idiot, unable to understand what seemed like a cruel new language. But I did understand it.

'Shut up,' Tom said to them. 'Just shut up, why don't you.'

He made his way towards me again and put a protective arm around my shoulder. Raging, I shrugged him off. He was quite drunk and he almost fell. When he found his balance, his eyes had gone cold. 'Fine!' he shouted, waving a can of something in the air. 'Be a bitch if you want to. But you might want to know that your best friend is off riding your precious Tony behind your back.'

The guitar music stopped. The whole night fell into a solid silence. The group on the beach suddenly looked like a photograph, black and white and unmoving. Out of nowhere, Nessa and Eve appeared. One stood on either side of me.

'That's enough, Tom,' Nessa said. At least I think it was Nessa. She was always louder than Eve..

I could not move. My legs did not respond to my urgent need to take flight. My whole body seemed to have shut down. And then, suddenly, I was walking.

To be more accurate, I was being walked by Nessa and Eve back up the slope and into the hotel grounds. Neither of them had said a word. Finally, I could speak.

'Is it true?'

Patricia's words were still alive in my ear. I could still see Tom's face in my mind. My brain started to make connections, some of them going back weeks. Everything inside my head started going off in all directions. I pressed my hands to my head to stop the noise inside.

'I think so,' Nessa said.

'But we're not sure,' Eve said. 'You will need to ask her.'

I moved away from them, walking backwards. I warded them off the same way I had warded off Patricia and her words.

'I'm okay,' I said. 'Go back to your party. I'm okay.' And then I fled. There is no other word for it. I think I heard them calling after me, but I'm not sure. I ran in the direction of the boys' block, taking the long way round. I didn't want to pass through the staff kitchen again. I didn't want to see Patricia's troubled look, didn't want to hear her words of comfort. Besides, this way I could keep to the shadows and my approach would not be heard.

A bedroom door opened outwards. I stood back. I knew which room was Tony's. He shared the second to last prefab with Gerry. They got a room each. I had spent many hours thinking about being in there with Tony, the two of us curled up together. As I watched, you both emerged, the light from the room casting a slowly growing shape onto the grass. He had you in his arms, pulled close to him. Your arms were wrapped around his neck.

There was no mistaking what I saw. You kissed. It was a lovers' kiss, and I cried out at last.

★

The rest is very clear.

I ran like someone possessed back down to the beach, my arms out in front of me, my face drenched with tears. Tom didn't even blink. I ran right into his arms and we fell onto the sand, hands tearing at each other, mouths locked together. When the anger drifted away, the pleasure was intense and unexpected.

'I'm so glad,' he whispered. The others had all gone by then. We had the beach to ourselves. 'I have wanted this for ages.'

I scrambled to my feet. 'I have to go,' I said. My fingers trembled as I tried to do up the buttons on my blouse.

'What?' he looked confused. 'What's wrong?'

'I have to go.' What else could I say? That I couldn't bear to see him, to see any of them? That they were all reminders of my humiliation? I left him there, his calls ringing in my ears as I stumbled back up the beach.

I didn't even pack. I ran all the way back to the village for the night bus to Dublin. I caught it with seconds to spare.

When I got home, my father opened the door. His face was crumpled and stained with tears. 'How did you get here?' he asked. 'I've only just spoken to Patricia. How did you get here so fast?'

'It does not matter,' I said, pushing past him. Something in the house felt wrong. Suddenly terrified, I asked him. 'What's happened?'

Mother's stroke is what happened, earlier that night, probably around the time I was falling into Tom's arms. Guilt ambushed me. This was my punishment. I deserved to feel bad. I had forgotten Mother's first rule. The one about keeping boys at arm's length, about keeping their respect.

And when I saw her in the hospital the following day, I knew that all her words were true. She could not spare me, not then, not ever.

The twins' faces were white masks, their eyes blue and wide and uncertain. 'When will Mammy be better?' Joey and Barney clung to me that night. They clung in all the months that followed too.

★

When Mother came home, unable to speak or look after even her most basic needs, Dad nursed her with a tenderness that made me cry. There was no question of my going back to school. Dad needed me at home. Mother needed me at home. The twins had to be minded, mothered, comforted.

She lived another fifteen years, my mother. Her days were a slow trail from bed to kitchen, cups of tea drunk through straws, meals fed to her with a spoon. We bought twin beds for downstairs. One for her, one for me. Dad continued to go to work, his once strong self suddenly weakened. We survived, we all did. We lived quietly, with the sound turned down.

Dad lived until just before last Christmas. He turned ninety-five in November. The night he died, he turned to me and took my hand. 'You have a heart of gold,' he said. His thin fingers patted mine. 'You are a good girl.'

A good girl, fifty-five and a half years of age.

A couple of days after my escape, Patricia arrived with my suitcase. We did not speak of the things she had told me about you. She drove to see my father and me two or three more times, and then stopped. On her last visit to the house, I could hear her in the hall with my father, her whispering low and urgent. At least once, I was sure that I heard the sudden catch of a sob. I heard my father's voice then. Just one firm word. 'No.'

I never saw Patricia again.

Chapter Nine

I have turned out to be a dab hand at computers. That is how I have kept in touch with things for all these years. Dad used to call the laptop my window to the world.

I found Tom's email address a couple of years back. At least, I'm almost sure it was his. The man in the tiny photo was so like him, even after almost four decades. It seemed that the longer I looked at his photograph, the more I could make out his teenage features. The years melted away, leaving the gangly teenager I had known. I wrote to him, asking if he remembered me. I got no reply. I am not even sure what I would have said to him if he had written back. His thin face has haunted me on and off over the years. I would have liked his forgiveness.

And of course, I've googled you on several occasions. O'Carroll, Dr Marie-Claire. I've kept up with your stellar career. A psychiatrist, no less. You fix people's lives. But you have not been all that good at fixing your own, have you? Married for the third time. Divorced twice. Once in 1995 and again in 2005. You have three grown-up children. Two boys and a girl. I saw your photo in the paper a few months ago. Some award you had received. I was curious, of course. I wanted to see what you and your family looked like. Your children surrounded you, but there was no sign of a husband. I have written to you several times over the years, by the way, but never posted any of the letters. Perhaps I will now, this last time. You may remember that you wrote to me, too, just the once, around the middle of that memorable August. You wrote about how you had never planned to fall in love with Tony. And about how you never meant to hurt me, how you were going to tell me eventually, but that things were 'complicated'.

Complicated. Was that what had made Matt 'complicated', by the way? Had you stolen him, too? Perhaps you had meant to explain. Perhaps not. It no longer matters. All I know is that the life I had begun to grasp escaped me that night.

Not Tony. God knows I would have got over him. In fact, I hardly gave him a second thought. But I had believed that our friendship was solid, unbreakable. I believed that we would be part of each other's lives forever. You had shown me the sort of future that I might have had. You made me brave.

When you left, I discovered something. I found that I could no longer fly.

★

I have been on my own, clearly, for all these years. But I have joined several online dating agencies since Dad died, mostly out of curiosity. I wanted to see what happened to other people to make them end up like me. It's been an interesting process. I've had some nice cups of coffee, a few visits to the cinema or the theatre. I have also met some total nutters, it has to be said. But recently I met someone special.

We stumbled across each other through one of my more expensive dating agencies. He's a few years older than I am, which is always a good thing in a man. Our profiles were matched instantly. He often talks about how much we have in common.

When we first met, I was careful. I wasn't sure what to expect. But the poor man was heartbroken because his wife had cheated on him. He was in need of a good female partner. His sense of betrayal was clear that first night. And with that, all of my nerves disappeared. This was something I knew well. This was emotion I could handle.

I did all the right things. I listened, I didn't judge and I took things slowly. I have tried not to influence him, of course. Over the last few months, I have paid attention. I was even able to look surprised when he told me his wife's name.

'My goodness,' I said. 'I used to know someone with that name, but it's almost forty years ago. It can't possibly be the same person.'

We were sitting in my living room. I had lit the fire to make the room cosy. It was mid-April, but the evening was chilly. I had the central heating on too. We had supper laid out on the coffee table and we were sipping a good, chilled white wine.

'Really?' he said. 'You did? I wonder could it possibly be her?' He was all eagerness then. He wanted to know everything. We took our wine glasses up to my study, it used to be the room that Joey and Barney shared. It is a big room at the back of the house. My photograph albums were arranged neatly on my bookshelves. I ran my finger along them and chose the one labelled 'Summer 1973'.

I showed him the photos of Athlone, of the boys surrounding you in that Galway pub. David could not believe the coincidence. As I said, I managed to look surprised. And I told him everything.

We spent that whole evening looking at photos and sharing memories. Your husband is a gentle soul. Trusting and generous. He deserves better. He has had enough this time, he says. No more forgiveness. This time, he is leaving you high and dry.

I am meeting him again tonight.

★

This afternoon, I took my two grand-nieces and two grand-nephews to the beach where the hotel used to be. It is still the same, with the same bright sand, the same graceful curve. There is a new, better shop where the post office once stood.

The fishing boats had just come in and the fishermen offered the children some mackerel to feed the seals. Young Orla was the bravest. She took the shiny fish with its small heart still beating. I have great hopes for Orla.

'Throw it high,' one of the fishermen said. 'The seals will jump to catch it. Trust me, they won't miss.' He said the seals have come back to the harbour, perhaps following some mysterious instinct of their own. Orla, Emma and I sat together on the harbour wall, swinging our legs and eating choc-ices. Emma squealed as the seals caught the flying fish that Orla threw. Their huge bodies were graceful in the water.

'Look, Auntie Miriam! Look at the way they can jump so high!'

The boys skimmed stones on the other side of the harbour wall. Joe and Bernard Junior were just like their grandfathers as they tried being cool.

When we were done, I drove home along the coast. The sky was red as we reached Dublin, the evening clouds lighting up in the glorious sunset. It had been a perfect day so far.

I left them home an hour or so ago and came home to change and get ready for tonight. David likes my cooking. He is not one for fancy restaurants. And so we will eat dinner and listen to music and talk about the books we are reading. We will also talk about you.

And then we will continue making plans, looking forward, shaping our future together.